"We'll never get to solve a crime!"

Dottie said as she kicked a pebble along the sidewalk. "Nothing ever happens in dumb old Dozerville."

"She's right," Jay agreed. "Chief Klink already caught most of the crime bosses, the super spies, and the criminal geniuses."

"And the Dozerville police catch all the leftover crooks," said Lee.

Dottie kicked another pebble down the street. "Like I said—nothing ever happens here."

"Well, we just have to keep looking," said Jimmy. "Stay alert for anything strange or suspicious. Anything that marks the trail to mystery."

Suddenly, T.J. pointed to something just ahead of them. "I think that trail to mystery is shorter than you think. Look!"

THE CASE OF
The Funny Money Man

•

William Alexander

•

Troll Associates

Cover art: Judith Sutton
Illustrated by: Dave Henderson

Library of Congress Cataloging-in-Publication Data

Alexander, William, (date)
    The case of the funny money man / William Alexander.
        p.   cm.—(The Clues kids; #1)
        Summary: The Clues Kids, five foster children living with Chief
    Klink and his wife, suspect their new neighbors of being
    counterfeiters.
        ISBN 0-8167-1692-7 (lib. bdg.)   ISBN 0-8167-1693-5 (pbk.)
        [1. Mystery and detective stories.   2. Foster home care—Fiction.]
    I. Title.   II. Series: Alexander, William.   The Clues kids; #1.
    PZ7.A3786Cas   1990
    [Fic]—dc20   89-36358

A TROLL BOOK, published by Troll Associates,
Mahwah, NJ 07430

Copyright © 1990 by Troll Associates, Mahwah, New Jersey

Printed in the United States of America.

10 9 8 7 6 5 4 3 2 1

JAY LOCKE

<u>Code name:</u> Clicker—Jay takes the pictures...lots of pictures. No clue escapes his lens because he shoots everything—windows, pets, doorknobs, lint—everything.

T.J. BOOKER

<u>Code name:</u> Smoke Screen—T.J. is the greatest disguise artist in the world (he asked me to say that). Actually, he *does* make up some great disguises. Some of them are pretty strange...but that's T.J.

JIMMY LOCKE

<u>Code name:</u> Jaws—He's the information man. He asks the questions. With his razor-sharp mind (he *made* me say that), Jimmy can break down any suspect.

DOTTIE BREWSTER

<u>Code name:</u> Short Stuff—She's the normal one of the bunch. Dottie looks for clues, tails crooks, keeps track of their fees, and tries to keep the others out of trouble. That's harder than you think!

LEE VAN THO

<u>Code name:</u> Smudge—Lee gets the fingerprints. He *really* gets the fingerprints. He usually makes a mess getting the prints, but he gets them!

C·H·A·P·T·E·R
1

*T*his is the town of Dozerville, Illinois, population 12,533 and one half. The town census taker, Amos Note-worthy, gave half citizenship to his pet chimp, Boswell. But that's another story.

There are three banks, a shopping mall, and the Dozerville post office. There are also two libraries, several toy stores, a quad movie theater, and twenty-six pizza parlors. The townspeople like a lot of pizza. Extra cheese, no anchovies. But that's another story, too.

Dozerville is a friendly, quiet, peace-loving community. It's safe because of two ever-vigilant forces. One can be found next door to the Town Hall—that's the police department. The other can be found at the Wrighter Ele-mentary School. Its members carry schoolbooks. One of them packs a pocket full of chocolate-covered raisins. And *that* story begins here.

"Come on! It's almost *Cosmic Cop* time!" yelled twelve-year-old Jay Locke. Jay ran down the school steps with fifty other children.

"We've got a half hour to get home before the show starts!" he said.

"I'm right behind you!" replied Jimmy, Jay's twin brother.

The two boys were identical in every way except for the way Jimmy combed his sandy brown hair. And the kinds of food he liked to eat. And the way he wore his clothes. Well— their faces were the same, anyway.

It was a chilly Monday afternoon, the early part of autumn. Bright red and yellow leaves were falling everywhere.

Jay and Jimmy ran across the schoolyard and stopped by a low stone wall. A big cardboard box was propped beside it. The word "wastebasket" was painted on the side of the box, and it seemed filled with crumpled newspapers and leaves. It looked a little weird, but the boys were too excited to pay any attention.

"Today Cosmic Cop takes on a brand new case," Jay exclaimed. Besides being the best cartoon hero, Cosmic Cop was the boys' favorite detective. He was a galactic peace officer dedicated to stopping crime in its tracks— or at least slowing it down a little.

"I know," Jimmy replied eagerly. He pulled a small notepad from his Windbreaker. "According to my information Cosmic is going after the galaxy's greatest criminal genius—"

"Bad Penny Slade," yelled a young Vietnamese boy as he ran up to them.

This was Lee Van Tho, Jimmy and Jay's eleven-year-old foster brother.

As Lee ran his fingers through his long black hair, Jay and Jimmy noticed smudges on his face and hands. There were even blotches on his clothes.

"You've got ink stains all over you," said Jimmy. "Have you been trying to fingerprint the science lab rabbits again?"

"No." Lee looked down at his sneakers. "The frogs."

The twins burst out laughing. Oddly enough, the cardboard wastebasket began to jiggle.

"At least I don't talk everybody to death!" said Lee, pointing a smudge-covered finger at Jimmy.

"And I don't take dumb pictures of everything that moves!" he said, turning toward Jay.

"It doesn't hurt to take pictures of possible suspects," Jay grumbled.

Lee folded his arms across his chest. "Since when is a kneecap a suspect?" he asked.

"Since the kneecap belonged to a suspected spy!" Jay shouted.

"Oh, brother," said a little voice from nowhere. "That *spy* turned out to be the school principal, picking up his laundry."

Jimmy, Jay, and Lee suddenly stopped arguing and looked around.

"Over here," the voice said impatiently.

Quickly the boys turned and leaned over the stone wall.

The cardboard box leaned too.

There, sitting on the grass, was a little girl in jeans and a sweat shirt.

"Dottie," said Jimmy. "How long have you been sitting there?"

Dottie looked at her watch. "Ten minutes and thirteen seconds," she replied. "I got here exactly five minutes before you."

This was their foster sister, Dottie Brewster. She was eight years old, with long, curly red hair and big green eyes.

It didn't bother the boys that Dottie *thought* she was always right. It bothered them that she *was* right—usually.

Dottie jumped up and grabbed her backpack. "We'd better hurry if we want to get home before *Cosmic Cop* starts."

"We know that," said Jay as he helped Dottie over the wall. "But we've got to wait for T.J."

"He's already here," Dottie replied.

"Where?" asked Lee.

"Here!" shouted a voice from inside the box. A thin black boy jumped out of the box, scattering papers everywhere. This was T. J. Booker, master disguise artist. He was ten years old and the fifth member of the family.

"He was here all the time," said Dottie. "*Now* can we go home?"

A few minutes later the kids were hurrying along the streets of Dozerville. They passed

the local supermarket, the video store, and the pet shop. They also passed three pizza parlors.

"T.J., that was a pretty good disguise," said Jimmy as they ran down Upton Street. "It was almost as good as the one Cosmic Cop used in—"

"I know, I know," T.J. interrupted. "Wait'll you see the one I'm working on now. I've got it stashed in my room."

"I can't believe I have a *room*," said Dottie. "My *own* room."

"Yeah," said Jay. He pulled his camera from his pocket. "I know what you mean. We *all* have our own rooms."

"It sure beats living in a shelter," said T.J. He thought back to his days at the County Children's Shelter, where he had shared a big room with ten other boys. The people at the shelter had been kind to him, but it was nothing like a real home.

"And we owe it all to the Klinks," Jimmy added. "Without them Jay and I might have been sent to live in different homes. We might never have seen each other again."

"I still don't believe they took us all," Jay said.

"Guess you're right," Lee agreed. "After all, Mr. and Mrs. Klink came for only one kid. But then they saw Jay, and Jimmy was his brother, and I was Jimmy's best friend, and T.J. was Jay's—"

"And then Dottie began to cry," T.J. added.

"So they took all of us—a package deal," Dottie grinned.

T.J. nodded. "The Chief said it was his chance to have a family basketball team."

Phil and Patty Klink were the kids' foster parents. They had volunteered to let homeless children live with them. They had chosen to give these five kids food, clothing, and love—to care for them so they wouldn't feel unwanted.

Phil had been chief of police until he retired. He'd been good at his job, and even now the police still called him for advice. His wife, Patty, was one of the most active members on the community board. She was always doing something to help people and to better the town.

But no matter how busy they were, Phil and Patty always had time for the kids. The Klinks made Jay, Jimmy, Lee, Dottie, and T.J. feel like one big family.

"I'm just sorry we didn't live with them when the Chief was on the force," said Jimmy. All the kids called Phil Klink "the Chief."

"He sure solved a lot of big cases," said Jay. *Click.* He took a picture of Mrs. Minnelli, with her hair in curlers, putting out the trash. She wasn't happy about that.

"He would have solved a lot more cases," said Lee proudly, "if I'd been there with my fingerprinting stuff."

"Or me with my camera," said Jay.

"Or me with my disguises," T.J. said eagerly.

Jimmy suddenly jumped in front of the other kids and dropped his schoolbooks.

"Or me," he declared. "With my *natural* ability to dig up facts." The kids stopped and stared at him. "With my untapped talent to grill suspects until they break out in a cold sweat." He began circling the others. "Their willpower bending under the hypnotic gaze of my steely blue eyes—"

"They're brown like mine," Jay corrected.

"Blue sounds better," Jimmy replied quickly. "Grilling them until—"

"Gag it, Jimmy!" the other kids shouted together.

"Man, they should call you Jaws," said T.J.

"You're just jealous because I'm a born detective," Jimmy declared.

"It doesn't matter if we're good detectives or not." Dottie kicked a pebble along the sidewalk. "We'll never get to solve a crime. Nothing ever happens in dumb old Dozerville."

"She's right," Jay agreed. "Mr. Klink already caught most of the crime bosses, super spies, and criminal geniuses."

"And the Dozerville police catch all the leftover crooks," said Lee.

Dottie kicked another pebble down the street. "Like I said, nothing ever happens here."

The kids were still talking about crooks and crime when they turned the corner onto their street. Webb Avenue was lined with old trees and beautiful homes.

"Well, we just have to keep looking," said Jimmy. "Stay alert for anything strange, or suspicious—anything that marks the trail to mystery."

Suddenly Lee pointed to something just ahead of them. "I think that trail to mystery is shorter than you think. Look!"

C·H·A·P·T·E·R
2

*L*ee was pointing at a scene taking place halfway down the street.

A large moving van was parked by a small brown house. The truck's loading ramp was sticking out and furniture and boxes were scattered everywhere.

The sign on the van read "Three Guys and a Truck. We'll move anything—once."

A tall, thin man was standing near the van, waving his arms wildly. With his long nose and wide eyes, he looked like a dancing pelican.

"I wonder why he's acting so weird," said Lee. "Maybe they're stealing stuff from that house."

T.J. chuckled. "I doubt it. Nobody lives there. Let's check it out anyway."

"Somebody's moving *in*," said Jay as they reached the van.

The moving men were unloading a large, expensive-looking cabinet made mostly of glass. Two of the men were trying to balance the cabinet on the third man's back. This might have been easier to do if he hadn't been crawling on his hands and knees. It was even more difficult because the men kept yelling at each other as they inched down the ramp.

"I got it!"

"You got it?"

"Yeah, I got it. Wait!"

"What?"

"I don't got it!"

The kids watched as the thin man tried to plead with the movers. "Please, gentlemen— I'm sure my wife will find the front door key soon. Then you can carry these things *inside*."

"He must be the new owner," Jimmy whispered to the others.

"Don't worry about a thing," said the mover with the long dark hair. "We're experts."

The mover with the cabinet on his back tried to look up. "Yeah," he grunted. "We've been doing this for at least—two whole days."

The new owner moaned and put his head in his hands.

Just then a car drove up next to the van. A very thin woman jumped out and hurried up to the front of the house. "I found the keys," she shouted as she reached the door.

"Great!" said the mover with the long hair. "We can take this cabinet right inside."

"It'll be a cinch," said one of his partners.

Slowly the three men eased the cabinet off the truck and on to the sidewalk. Seconds later they were staggering and stumbling toward the house.

The new owner seemed to notice the children for the first time. He gave them a friendly smile.

"Hi," said Dottie. "I'm Dottie Brewster and these are my brothers." She pointed to the boys.

"I'm pleased to meet you. I'm—" The man's introduction stopped short when he noticed the boys. "Did you say these are your— brothers?"

"That's right," said Dottie. "Jimmy, Jay, Lee, and T.J." She pointed to each boy as she said his name.

"We live with the Klinks in that big white house across the street," Jay said.

"We're adopted, kind of," said Lee.

"I see." The man still looked very puzzled.

"Are you moving in?" asked Jimmy.

"No," Lee replied with a smirk on his face. "They're having a yard sale."

"Boys." Dottie sighed.

Just then the woman came out of the house. "Well," she called out as she came down the path. "Who do we have here?"

"These are the uh—uh," the man stammered. "I mean, all of them are, uh, uh—"

"We're the Klinks' kids," said Jay. "We're your neighbors."

"Oh," the woman said. "We're the Greenes. My name is Olive and this is my husband, Forrest."

"Welcome to the neighborhood," Jimmy said politely.

Just then the movers rushed out of the house and picked up a few more boxes.

"Hurry up and toss this stuff inside," one of them grumbled. "We've got plenty more to go." Staggering, the three men headed back into the house.

"*Toss?*" Mr. Greene's voice quivered as he spoke. "Did he say toss?"

"Yep," Jimmy replied cheerfully. "He sure did. I think they—

"Excuse us, kids," said Mrs. Greene as she and her husband hurried up the walkway.

"Boy," said T.J. "The Greenes sure looked worried."

"You would be, too, if those bozos were moving your stuff," said Dottie.

Meanwhile, Jay had moved closer to the van. "Look, you guys," he said. "Why don't we give the Greenes a hand? We could carry some of this stuff inside for them."

"Are you nuts?" Lee exclaimed. "We'll miss *Cosmic Cop.*"

"No, we won't," Jay replied. "We've got ten minutes before it starts."

"Eight minutes and fifteen seconds," Dottie corrected him.

"Come on," Jay said, ignoring her. He ran up the loading ramp into the truck. "We can carry some of the small stuff."

The others grumbled as they put down their schoolbooks. "All right," said Jimmy, stepping up to the van. "But just for a few minutes."

"Great," said Jay. He quickly began handing down small boxes and bundles. "It'll be easy," he said cheerfully. "The movers have already taken out all the big stuff."

After loading Jimmy with pillows and things, Jay handed a few items to T.J. "That's enough," he said. "I'll get this thing by myself."

The thing was a large stuffed duck. It was almost as big as Jay was, and it wore a bright yellow sweat shirt with "Danger Duck" written in large red letters. Jay went over and picked it up. It was heavier than he had expected.

"Are you sure you can handle that?" asked T.J. As long as he'd known Jay, his foster brother had always been a klutz.

"No problem," Jay replied, trying to see over the duck's shoulder. He took a couple of unsteady steps forward. "Just tell me where the ramp is."

"It's right—"

"What are you doing?" shouted a high-pitched voice.

T.J. and Dottie turned to see Mrs. Greene rushing down the walkway. She looked very upset.

"Please put that down," she called out.

"Don't worry," said Jay as he stepped forward. "I've got it all under contro —"Jay's sentence was cut short as he missed the ramp and stepped out into midair. As he fell forward, just missing T.J., the duck caught on the edge of the ramp.

There was a loud tearing sound, and Jay and the duck hit the ground. Luckily Jay was on top.

"Are you all right?" asked Mrs. Greene as she ran over to Jay.

Jay stood up and started brushing himself off. "Don't worry," he said. "I didn't break anything."

"Yes, you did," said Dottie, pointing at the ground. "You broke the duck—and look what's inside."

Jay looked down at the stuffed animal. Its left side had been torn open. And pouring out was a different kind of stuffing. Money! Packages of twenty-dollar bills—what looked like thousands of dollars!

C·H·A·P·T·E·R
3

"**W**ow!" Lee shouted. "That duck is full of money!"

"Yeah," said T.J. "Duck bucks."

Before either of them could say another word, Mrs. Greene quickly stuffed the money back in the hole. Then she scooped the duck into her arms.

"Don't worry about a thing," she said nervously. She held the stuffed toy very tightly, hiding the torn section. "I'm sure the tear can be fixed easily."

T.J. looked confused. "But what about the duck bucks?"

"That's right," said Dottie. "Can we see the money?"

"Money?" said Mr. Greene as he hurried to his wife's side. "What money?"

"We just saw a whole lot of money sticking out of your duck," said Jimmy.

Mr. Greene chuckled. It was a funny kind of chuckle, the I-have-to-stall-for-a-few-seconds-until-I-figure-out-what-I'm-going-to-say kind. "Nonsense," said Mr. Greene. It was the best he could come up with. "That was just the stuffing you saw."

"Stuffing?" Jay exclaimed.

"Yes," said Mrs. Greene, still hugging the duck like a long-lost friend. "That's what it was. Green stuffing."

"Very green," said her husband.

"Stuffing, huh?" T.J. said suspiciously. "Boy, I'd sure like to eat at your house on Thanksgiving."

"Maybe you can," Mr. Greene stuttered. "Uh, sometime." He began nudging his wife toward their home. "But right now we have a lot of work to do."

Dottie started after the Greenes. "Wait a minute," she said. "I know we saw—"

Just then they all heard one of the movers shouting in the house. "I said drop that thing and give me a hand!"

There was a loud crash.

"Oh, no," moaned Mr. Greene. He began rushing up the walkway. "Excuse us, kids."

"Yes, excuse us," Mrs. Greene called out as she followed her husband into the house.

Jay looked at the others. He could see that each of them shared the same thought.

"There's something weird about our new

neighbors," Jay said. "And I think we should find out what it is."

"Not now," said Lee as he grabbed up his schoolbag. "*Cosmic Cop* starts in—"

"Two minutes!" shouted Dottie. She was already racing across the street.

"Come on," Jimmy called to the others. "We can talk about the Greenes later. Let's go!"

The boys ran across the street and followed Dottie into the house.

The Klinks' home was old—over a hundred years old, to be exact. It stood three stories high, with eleven rooms, a creepy old attic, and a huge stone cellar. There was even a large barn attached to one side of the house.

The building had a few drafts, leaks, creaks, and moans. But basically it was solid—dependable. Just like the Klinks.

One hour after meeting the Greenes, the kids were sitting down to dinner in the kitchen. Phil Klink had just placed the main course on the table.

He was a tall, heavyset man in his late fifties. His hair was white and wavy. His mustache was big, bushy, and always getting into his food.

"All right, kids," said Phil, looking at the platter of meat loaf. "Your mother says I'm putting on a little too much weight. So you'll have to eat most of this."

Just as Phil sat down, Patty Klink walked

into the room. Mrs. Klink was a small woman with sparkling blue eyes and short red hair with only "a touch of gray," as she was fond of saying. And she had a friendly expression that made her look as if she were always smiling. Except now, that is. Patty Klink looked annoyed, and she appeared to be holding something behind her back.

"Lee," said Mrs. Klink. "Guess what I just found in the linen closet."

"Uh . . . linen?" Lee said sheepishly. He knew something was wrong.

"That's right." Mrs. Klink walked toward the table, still holding her hands behind her. "Linen that looks like this." She held up a dishtowel and some cloth napkins. They were covered with black stains.

"These look like the paw prints of a dog to me," Mrs. Klink continued.

"A dog?" Lee asked, trying to sound innocent. "You mean Snoop?"

A tiny whine came from under the table. It was Snoop, the Klinks' basset hound. The large, floppy-eared pooch peeked out and looked up at Mrs. Klink with her sorrowful brown eyes.

"She's the only dog we have," Patty Klink replied without looking down.

Lee tried to smile. "Gee, you know Snoop likes to sleep in the linen closet."

"But usually she doesn't have ink all over her paws," said Mrs. Klink.

"I was just—"

"I know, Lee." Mrs. Klink dropped the soiled linen in his lap. "You were just practicing your fingerprinting techniques. Well, right after dinner you can practice your clean-up techniques."

"Yes, ma'am," Lee said with a heavy sigh.

"Fine," said Mrs. Klink, sitting down in her chair. "Now let's eat our dinner. Tonight there's a meeting to discuss better housing for the elderly. I don't want to miss it."

For the first few minutes the kids talked about their favorite subject.

"Wow," said Jimmy. "Cosmic Cop will never get out of that trap."

"What a way to go," said T.J. "Trapped in a giant intergalactic hole-punching doughnut maker."

"He'll get out of it," Dottie said. She was trying to hide her asparagus under her mashed potatoes.

"He'll probably use his official Galactic Police pocket-size, remote-controlled, solar-powered, dyno-dimensional battering ram," she said all in one breath. "You know, the one that matches his gold uniform with the silver and black trim."

"Then he'll find out what Bad Penny Slade is up to," said Lee. *His* asparagus was mysteriously disappearing under the table.

"I'd like to find out what Mr. and Mrs. Greene are up to," said Jay, swallowing his food quickly. "They sure acted weird this afternoon."

"Do you know anything about them, Chief?" asked Jimmy.

Phil wiped a bit of gravy from his mustache and looked at Jimmy with a curious expression on his face. "I know that they just moved here from Walkerton," he said. "I know that they just bought the house across the street. And . . . that they wouldn't like five curious kids snooping into their personal business."

"We don't snoop," T.J. said defensively. "We just—uh—"

"Investigate," Jimmy declared.

"And embarrass yourselves," Phil Klink added. "Do you remember when you suspected Mr. Dellwood of being a jewel thief?"

Dottie placed her hand on her foster father's arm. "But you said he was a thief!"

"When did I ever say that?" Phil Klink looked confused.

"You said with the prices he charged he was the biggest crook around," Dottie replied.

Patty Klink chuckled into her napkin.

"Well, I didn't mean he was a real crook exactly," Phil mumbled. "I meant—well—never mind. Just don't—"

"I know," Jimmy said quickly. "Don't snoop. We'll leave the Greenes alone."

Jay was about to disagree until Jimmy signaled him to keep quiet.

The Klinks spent the rest of their dinnertime talking about really important stuff. Like bossy teachers, nosy neighbors, and who squeezes the toothpaste from the middle of the tube.

After they'd finished dinner and cleaned the kitchen (and the linen closet), the kids raced to their private clubhouse. It was up in the old hayloft in the back of their barn.

The clubhouse was filled with a lot of great junk the kids had collected. They'd made a desk from an old door and a couple of milk crates. There were a few creaking chairs and big pillows to sit on. And they had all their toys and disguises right where they wanted them—everywhere.

"I bet the Greenes are like the man in that old movie." Jimmy sat absent-mindedly tapping a small wooden hammer on the desk. "He didn't trust banks, so he put all his money in his mattress."

"But the Greenes put their money in a duck," Dottie corrected him. "Not a mattress." She was curled up on a big pile of pillows, combing the fur on a stuffed animal.

"I think the Greenes are spies." Jay flopped down on an old chair that swayed alarmingly.

"Spies?" Lee said, amazed.

"Sure," said Jay. He began looking through a photo album full of pictures he'd taken of suspicious people. To Jay, that meant anybody that moved. "I bet they're here to buy some secret formula from a foreign agent."

"You're both wrong," T.J. declared. "The Greenes are part of the mob."

"Oh, brother," Dottie moaned.

"Nah," said Lee. "They're part of a bank robbery gang. They split up the loot from their last job. Now they have to lay low—until the heat's off."

"Maybe so," said Jimmy. "But whatever they are, we've got to watch them, tail them, grill 'em."

"Yeah," Jay agreed. He tossed the photo album on the desk. "Photograph every move they make."

"That's a lot of film," Dottie chuckled.

Lee started checking his fingerprinting kit. "I'll get their prints and send them to the FBI."

"This I've got to see," said Dottie.

Jimmy slammed the hammer on the desk. "Then it's settled! We go after the Greenes."

"I say we start tomorrow." Jay jumped to his feet. "The Greenes are our first big case, and nothing's going to stop us. Absolutely nothing."

It was a great moment.

"Kids," Patty Klink called from the house. "Time to hit those homework assignments."

Sometimes parents can ruin a great moment.

The next day went quickly. The kids couldn't stop thinking about the Greenes—which made it hard on their teachers. Even Dottie had trouble concentrating on her schoolwork. And when three o'clock came around, she was one of the first kids out of the building.

She made her way to the low stone wall

and sat down on the grass. Her foster brothers were nowhere in sight.

"They're late again," Dottie said to herself. "They're always late."

Dottie leaned against the wall and gazed out across the street. She noticed a man walking up and down in front of the Dozerville First National Bank. It was Mr. DeVidus Cashton, the bank's vice president. Dottie knew Mr. Cashton because she had a savings account in his bank.

Usually, the vice president was a very calm, easygoing man. But Dottie noticed that he seemed really nervous today. He kept looking at his watch, looking up and down the street, and fingering a manila envelope in his hand.

Dottie was just wondering who or what he was waiting for when a woman in a trench coat joined Mr. Cashton. The woman had her back to Dottie, so she couldn't see who it was.

The two people talked for a few moments. Then the woman took something from Mr. Cashton. It looked like the manila envelope.

As the woman turned to go, Dottie got a good look at her face. She knew who the lady in the trench coat was—Mrs. Greene.

Dottie was shocked. Mrs. Greene was acting just as weird as Mr. Cashton. She looked up and down the street, then whispered something to the vice president.

Mr. Cashton gave a funny little nod, then

hurried into the bank. Mrs. Greene turned and walked away.

Dottie's mind was racing like a high-speed drill. She wondered why the two adults had been acting so strange.

Why was the vice president of her bank talking to a possible spy, mob member, and bank robber? What could they talk about— unless—

The idea hit her as hard as an invitation to summer school. The only thing a bank vice president and a thief could talk about was— robbing a bank!

C·H·A·P·T·E·R
4

When the boys arrived a few seconds later, Dottie was very excited.

"They're going to rob me," she said frantically. She quickly explained what had happened. "They're going to steal my money!"

"Yours, and a few other people's," said Jay.

"You don't understand!" Dottie twisted her hair nervously. "If we don't stop them, they'll get away with everything I have."

"All nine dollars and twenty-three cents," Jimmy said dryly.

Dottie's eyes blazed.

"Okay, okay," said Jay. "Let's fight about this later. Right now we have bigger problems. How are we going to find out what their plans are?"

T.J. quickly pulled a pair of dark glasses

and a floppy rainhat from his schoolbag. "We follow Mrs. Greene," he said, putting on his disguise. "That's how Cosmic would do it."

"Right," Jimmy agreed. "And the best way to do it is if we divide up, keeping twelve feet behind the suspect, and—"

"Gag it, Jimmy," Jay interrupted. "Let's just get going!"

The kids scrambled over the stone wall and raced along the street. In a matter of minutes they'd closed the gap between themselves and the mysterious Mrs. Greene.

"We've got only a half hour before *Cosmic Cop* starts," said Jimmy.

"This is more important," Lee said, breathing heavily.

"It sure is," T.J. agreed. He kept ducking behind people and things, attempting to go unnoticed by their suspect. Mrs. Greene may not have seen him—but everyone else sure did.

The kids moved along the winding streets of Dozerville. Like T.J., they dodged workmen, passers-by, and parking meters. Twice, Mrs. Greene turned and looked behind her— almost spotting the kids in hot pursuit. But somehow she never did see them.

Every now and then Mrs. Greene bought a few things. In a supermarket Jay took a picture of her in the frozen food section. Lee discovered it's messy trying to get fingerprints off ice-covered fish. And after a while the kids were getting pretty frustrated.

"This is going nowhere," said Jimmy. "So far, all she's done is spend money all over town."

"It's pretty boring, all right," said Dottie. "She hasn't done anything suspicious since she met with Mr. Cashton."

"Maybe we're on the wrong track," said T.J. He removed his glasses and cap. "Maybe she isn't up to anything at all."

"Oh, yeah?" said Jay. "Then look over there."

Just ahead, Mrs. Greene had stopped in front of a small store. The sign overhead read "Better Letter Printing Service. We're not sloppy. We just make copies."

"That's Mr. Letterman's shop," Jimmy exclaimed. "He prints posters and stuff for our school."

Just then a short, elderly man wearing a black apron and gold-rimmed eyeglasses stepped out of the store.

"And that's Mr. Letterman," said Jimmy. "He looks angry or something."

Mr. Letterman closed the door behind him. As he turned toward Mrs. Greene, he looked up and down the street.

The kids quickly ducked into a nearby doorway.

"That was close," Jay whispered.

"He's acting just like Mr. Cashton," said Dottie. She was squeezed between Jimmy and T.J.

"I know," Jay replied. He waited a few

seconds, then peeked out to see what was going on.

"What's happening?" Dottie asked.

"Mr. Letterman is talking to Mrs. Greene," said Jay.

"Is he still acting weird?" asked Lee.

"Yeah." Jay leaned back into the doorway. "And he's giving her something."

Dottie leaned out to take a look. "It looks like a big envelope—just like the one Mr. Cashton gave her."

"We're really on to something, guys!" Lee's eyes shone with excitement.

"I wish we could hear what they're saying," said Jay. He leaned out to take another peek.

T.J. pulled a woolen cap, earmuffs, and a bright orange scarf out of his bag. "Maybe we can. A master disguise artist is always ready."

"For what?" asked Jimmy. "A bad cold?"

"Very funny, smart guy." T.J. quickly put on his disguise. "Just watch a pro in action. I'll move like the wind. I'll blend into the scene like a ghost. I'll—"

"Get going and be careful," Dottie interrupted. She gave T.J. a little shove.

Pulling the scarf up over his mouth, T.J. stepped out of the doorway and began to move along the sidewalk. All his concentration was set on one thing—sneaking up on his target.

Finally he made it to a fruit and vegetable stand only a few feet from Mr. Letterman and Mrs. Greene.

T.J. grabbed a broom that was leaning against a fruit bin. He began sweeping the sidewalk, inching closer and closer—until he could hear what they were saying.

Mrs. Greene was smiling at the old printer. It was a strange smile. "The photographs make all the difference, Mr. Letterman," she said. "Without the pictures, my husband and I wouldn't be in business. Now, about payment—"

"You'll get the rest of the money after I've seen the product," said Mr. Letterman. His head twitched every time he spoke. T.J. couldn't tell if the store owner was nervous or had water in his ear.

"Very well," said Mrs. Greene. "I'll be back in two days. I'm sure you'll be happy to see me."

And with that Mrs. Greene turned and started down the street in the opposite direction. After Mr. Letterman went back into the store, T.J. ran back to join the others.

"I don't know what's going on," he said, "but she's got something he's going to buy from her."

"When?" asked Jay.

"In two days," T.J. replied.

Eagerly Jimmy began writing in his notebook. "Boy, we're on to something now!" he exclaimed.

"What?" asked Dottie. She crossed her arms and looked him in the eyes.

Jimmy stopped writing. "Uh, um, I don't know—yet."

"Then let's stay on her trail!" Lee shouted. "She might lead us to some real evidence."

The kids hurried down the street as fast as they could. They reached the corner in time to see Mrs. Greene turn into the Mini Mall parking garage.

"You think she's going for her car?" asked Jimmy.

Lee rolled his eyes. "No, she's probably going for her lawn mower."

Jay hurried toward the parking garage with the others hot on his heels. They caught up to him just as he started down the ramp. But when they reached the first level, Mrs. Greene was nowhere in sight. And neither was anyone else.

The kids moved slowly and cautiously along the narrow sidewalk that ran through the garage. The ramps twisted and turned, and wound around and off into the semidarkness. Neon lights threw ghostly shadows along the ground.

Their footsteps echoed faintly off the gray cement walls. And in the distance they could hear faint, creepy noises. But they didn't see Mrs. Greene. They didn't see another driver. And after a few seconds they didn't see the point in walking around in a parking garage—alone.

"This is spooky," said Lee. He inched closer to the other kids.

"It doesn't look like this when we come here with the Klinks," said Jay.

"That's because we're not alone then," said Jimmy.

"Well, we are now," Jay grumbled. "And it looks like we've lost our suspect."

"I think she went that way," said T.J. He pointed off toward a stairwell.

"Nah," Lee exclaimed. "She probably went over there." He gestured in another direction.

"She could have ducked out through an exit door," Jimmy said, looking around. "I think we passed a couple back there."

Jay sighed. "Like I said—I think we've lost her."

As her brothers tried to plan their next move, Dottie caught a glimpse of someone ducking around a pillar. But the person was too far off for her to see who it might be.

"Hey, guys," she said, trying to get their attention. "Jay, Jimmy, T.J.!"

But the boys were too busy talking to pay any attention to her.

"All right," she grumbled. "I'll do it myself." And off she went along the walkway.

Cautiously Dottie approached the area where she'd seen the figure. She tiptoed around the pillar and looked in all directions. Nothing. No Mrs. Greene. No car revving its engine, and no bright headlights.

Where had their mysterious new neighbor disappeared to?

Dottie walked down the ramp a little farther, then stopped. Ahead of her, the parking lot became even darker. The air was damp and musty smelling—like a room full of dirty gym socks.

"Lee was right," she said with a quiver in her voice. "This place *is* spooky."

Just as the nervous little girl turned to leave, she heard a rustling noise.

At first it was faint. But it grew louder. Something big was rushing toward her.

Dottie looked all around. *What should I do?* she thought.

She pressed up against a wall and listened as the sound grew louder—closer. Whatever it was, it was moving in her direction. Dottie knew it would be there very soon—and there was nowhere to hide.

C·H·A·P·T·E·R
5

*T*he sound grew louder, and suddenly something came rushing around the corner.

"Dottie!" it shouted.

Dottie screamed.

Then she realized that the *thing* was actually Jimmy, Jay, Lee, and T.J.

"You guys really scared me!" Dottie shouted. Though she was glad to see her brothers, Dottie didn't know whether to hug them or punch them in the nose.

"Why'd you go wandering off alone?" asked T.J. "We got worried."

"I thought I saw Mrs. Greene come around this corner," Dottie replied. "And you guys wouldn't listen to me."

Jay put his arm around her. "Hey, we're

sorry," he said. "But don't ever leave us like that. Promise?"

Dottie nodded.

Suddenly a man stepped out of a nearby door marked Maintenance Closet. "What are you kids doing here?" he asked.

"We were looking for—a—a—" Jay stammered.

"One of our teachers," Jimmy answered quickly. "We thought we saw her come this way."

"Well, there's nobody down here but us custodians," the man replied with a smile. "I just came to get some of my tools.

"Now, look," he continued. "You kids shouldn't be down here without your parents. Cars come and go all the time. You could get hurt."

"You're right, sir." Jay began leading the other kids out of the parking area. "Guess we should get home now. Good-bye."

"I'll come along just to make sure you get out all right." The custodian walked the kids to the entrance of the garage, then waved good-bye.

"We sure blew that one," said Jay when they were alone on the street. "We lost Mrs. Greene and we didn't learn anything about her plans to rob the bank."

"What do we do now?" asked T.J.

Jay looked at his watch. "I say we run home as fast as we can. *Cosmic Cop* starts in five minutes!"

"Maybe if we watch Cosmic, we'll get an idea how to handle our case!" Jimmy exclaimed. "Let's go!"

The electronic theme song of *Cosmic Cop* blared across the Klinks' living room.

Jay and Jimmy were stretched out on the couch, and T.J. was lying on the floor on top of several pillows. Sitting with his legs folded under him, Lee was very comfortable in Patty Klink's recliner. Dottie was all curled up in the Chief's overstuffed chair, nibbling on a rice cake.

"That was a weird episode," said Lee. He tossed a handful of chocolate-covered raisins into his mouth. "I wonder how Bad Penny Slade became rich all of a sudden."

"That's what Cosmic is trying to find out," said T.J., munching on a fudge-covered Kreme Kake. He leaned forward and turned off the TV.

"He'll do it too," said Lee. "All he has to do is get past that big fat Nova Beast. Piece of cake."

Dottie sighed and tucked herself even deeper into the chair. "We didn't learn anything from watching the show. Cosmic doesn't know what Bad Penny Slade is up to. And we don't know how to stop the Greenes from robbing my bank."

"Let's look at what we know so far," Jay said.

"Okay." Jimmy grabbed his notepad and

pencil from the coffee table. "We know that the Greenes have a duck full of money."

"Right," T.J. agreed. "And they don't want anybody to know about it."

Lee leaned forward in his chair. "And we know that they're going to rob the Dozerville First National Bank."

"We don't *know* that," Jay corrected him. "We only know that Mrs. Greene was talking to Mr. Cashton."

"*And* Mr. Letterman," Lee added. "But if they're planning to rob a bank, what do they need a printer for?"

"Who knows?" Dottie sighed.

Jimmy looked up from his notes. "Let's look at this mathematically," he said. "Let's look for the common denominator."

"That's what Sherlock Holmes always does," said Lee.

Jay chuckled. "So does my math teacher."

"Okay," said Jimmy. "What do Mr. Letterman and Mr. Cashton have in common?"

The room was quiet for a moment. The only sounds were crunching and munching.

Suddenly Dottie cried out, "Envelopes! They both had envelopes."

"What are you talking about?" Jimmy asked.

"Mr. Cashton gave Mrs. Greene a large envelope," said Dottie.

Jimmy snapped his fingers. "And so did Mr. Letterman!"

"But what was in the envelopes?" Lee asked.

T.J. licked the custard and chocolate from

his fingers, then reached for another Kreme Kake. He froze as he remembered the conversation he'd overheard.

"The pictures," he exclaimed. " 'My husband and I wouldn't be in business without them.' "

"What are you talking about?" asked Jimmy.

"That's what Mrs. Greene said to Mr. Letterman," T.J. replied. "She said something about some pictures. Then *he* said something about money."

Jay suddenly sat up straight. "Blackmail! That's what the Greenes are doing. I remember seeing it on an episode of *Cosmic*."

"Sure," said Jimmy. "I remember that episode. The victims passed money to the crook in an envelope."

Dottie bit down on a piece of rice cake. "But what does she have on them? I mean, what did Mr. Cashton do—cheat in a golf game or something?"

"I don't know about this blackmail idea," Jimmy said, puzzled. "What if we're wrong? What if the Greenes really are planning to rob the bank?"

The gang members looked at one another.

Finally Jay broke the silence. "There's only one way to find out what's really going on. We've got to watch the Greenes twenty-four hours a day."

"What do you mean *we*?" asked Dottie. "You don't mean we have to stay up all night?"

"Not all of us," Jay replied. "We'll take shifts."

"Sure," said Jimmy. There was excitement in his voice. "We can see their house from our bedroom windows."

"We'll start tonight, after dinner," Jay continued. "Lee, you go from seven to nine. Jimmy will take from nine to twelve. I'll go from twelve to three, Dottie from three to—"

Dottie sat up straight. "Forget it. I'm not sitting up all night."

"But—"

"No way." Dottie folded her arms and leaned back in the chair.

"Okay," said Jimmy. "Have it your way. T.J., you go from three to six."

"Then Dottie can go from six to eight," said Jay. He looked at his foster sister anxiously. She didn't say a word. "Come on, Dottie. We're trying to save *your* money, after all."

"Oh, all right," she grumbled.

"Great!" said Jimmy. "Then we're all set. Now we're ready for anything."

Just then they heard Phil Klink enter the house and head toward the living room. They quickly jammed snacks under pillows, magazines, and into their mouths.

When Phil entered the room he saw five angelic-looking children smiling up at him. He knew something was wrong.

"Well," he said, spotting the chocolate smears across their faces. "Who's ready for a *big* dinner?"

The kids stopped smiling.

That night—or morning, depending on how you feel about three A.M.—a bright silver-blue moon was shining down on a hundred-year-old house on Webb Avenue. And in a window of that house T.J. Booker nodded in and out of sleep. At least he did until he heard a strange sound—a low *click-fizz-snip* sound.

The sound floated over the Greenes' front lawn, across the street, and up to T.J.'s window. The ever-alert junior detective stirred—then listened. He could tell the sound was coming from the Greenes' garage. There was a soft yellow light shining through the side window.

"I've got to check it out," T.J. said with determination. He put on his jeans, shirt, and jacket, then grabbed a flashlight and quietly slipped out of his room.

Halfway down the hall he stopped. "No reason why I have to do this alone," he whispered to himself.

Five minutes later T.J. and a very sleepy Lee made their way along the hedges that ran next to the Greenes' garage.

"Why didn't Jimmy and Jay come with us?" Lee asked through a yawn.

"Because they're keeping watch from the house," T.J. whispered. "They'll call for help in case we need backup."

"That doesn't make me feel any better," Lee replied.

"Keep it down," said T.J. as they approached

the garage window. "All we have to do is take a peek inside, then run back and report. Now, come on."

The two boys inched their way up to the window. Inside, the garage was packed to the ceiling with boxes and tools and old furniture. The boys could see the Greenes standing next to a long workbench.

"It looks like anybody else's garage," Lee whispered. "Tools, old furniture, lumber, a printing press—"

"A printing press!" T.J. gasped.

Sure enough, Mr. and Mrs. Greene stood over a small printing press. Next to it was a photocopier, about the same size. But what was next to the copier really surprised the boys. Stacked in nice neat packets—

"Money!" T.J. rubbed his eyes, looked at Lee, and looked back through the window. "There must be thousands of dollars sitting on that table."

"And look where it's coming from." Lee pointed to Mrs. Greene. The slender young woman was pulling a crisp twenty-dollar bill out of the printing press.

She and Mr. Greene held the bill up to an overhead lamp. They examined it front and back—then smiled.

The boys ducked below the window and stared at each other.

"We were wrong about them," T.J. said as he grabbed Lee's arm. "They're not black-mailers or bank robbers."

"They're counterfeiters!" Lee wiped beads of sweat from his forehead. "Why steal money when you can make your own?"

"We've got to tell the others!" T.J. said. "Come on!"

Quickly the boys went around to the front of the garage. Their mission had been a success. Their first case was finally coming together.

Lee and T.J. moved carefully along the front of the garage, making their way back to the hedges. Unfortunately, T.J. wasn't moving as carefully as he should have been. He tripped over a garden hose and knocked over a stack of flowerpots. There was a loud crash . . . naturally.

Lee yanked T.J. to his feet. "Hurry up, before they hear us." He pulled him along—not noticing the metal pail or the garbage can. *Crash!*

"You think they heard that?" asked Lee as T.J. helped him up.

Before his foster brother could answer, they both felt a powerful hand clamp down on their shoulders.

"You boys shouldn't be out this late," said the quiet voice of Mr. Forrest Greene. "It could be dangerous. Very, very dangerous."

C·H·A·P·T·E·R
6

"*H*e's got them!" Jimmy dropped his binoculars and leaped from his bed. "Mr. Greene just caught Lee and T.J.! What are we going to do?"

"We get right over there—" Jay replied.

"Right," said Jimmy.

"After we wake up Dottie," Jay continued.

"Right," Jimmy agreed.

"And the Klinks."

"Wrong!" Jimmy exclaimed. "The Chief will roast us alive if he finds out!"

Jay looked Jimmy in the eyes. "You want to go after those guys alone?"

"We wake up the Chief," said Jimmy, grabbing his robe. "Let's go."

A parade of pajamas and bathrobes marched

through the chilly autumn air and across Webb Avenue.

Phil Klink was in the lead. The ex–police chief was used to late hours. He'd pulled a lot of all-night duty when he was on the force. And he was used to holding his temper in check until he had all the facts. Right now, though, the safety valve was cracking.

Patty Klink was always good-natured. But as they approached the Greenes' garage, Jimmy, Jay, and Dottie had a feeling nature was brewing a storm.

The group moved alongside the garage until they reached the window. Phil Klink peeked into the darkened interior.

"No lights, no Greenes, and no kids," he said. Though he spoke calmly, there was a hard edge to his voice. "You're sure you saw Mr. Greene grab them?"

"I sure did," Jimmy answered quickly.

"Let's try the house," Patty Klink suggested. She was holding Dottie's hand. The little girl could feel her foster mother trembling.

As they approached the Greenes' front door, Phil Klink signaled them to wait.

The kids were fascinated. Tonight they were seeing a different side of their foster father— the professional cop. His movements were sharp and quick. His eyes seemed to look everywhere at once, not missing a thing.

Phil Klink approached the front door. He took a deep breath, raised his hand to the doorknob, and—

The door popped open. There stood Mrs. Greene, holding a cup of hot chocolate and smiling from ear to ear.

"Come on in," she said cheerfully. "I thought I heard you coming up the walk. Forrest, look who's here."

Jimmy, Jay, and Dottie thought this was a signal for Mr. Greene to make some threatening move. So they burst into the house shouting, "Freeze, turkeys!"

The living room was filled with unpacked boxes and crates. But on one side there was a narrow couch covered with a wild plaid fabric. And sitting on that couch—hot chocolate in their hands—were T.J. and Lee.

"Hi, guys," they both said sheepishly. They lowered their heads when they saw the stern faces of their foster parents.

T.J. turned to Lee. "Drink up. I've got a feeling this is our last meal."

Explanations came fast and furious.

The Greenes explained how they had found the children out by the garage. The kids explained why they had been snooping around. And Phil explained to the kids what it meant to be "grounded for life."

"But, Chief," Jimmy pleaded. "The Greenes really are bank robbers!"

"No," Jay interrupted, "they're blackmailers!"

"You're both wrong," Lee shouted. "They're counterfeiters!"

Patty Klink took a deep breath. "Children,

you are making some very serious accusations. I don't—"

"But we can prove it," said T.J. "Make them show you the printing press and the money! Please, Chief!"

Just as Phil Klink was about to speak, Mr. Greene raised his hand. "I think I can straighten out this whole mess," he said, trying not to laugh. "Would you and the children follow me to the garage?"

"There you are," said Mr. Greene as he stood in front of the printing equipment. "Thousands of dollars worth of—"

"See," Lee interrupted. "We told you so."

"What do you call this?" Phil Klink asked, pointing at the stacks of money.

Mr. Greene smiled, "I call it Mug Money."

"What?" said the children.

"Mug Money," Mrs. Greene replied. She handed one of the bills to the kids. "As in mug shots. It looks pretty real, doesn't it?"

"The big difference is that we print the face of anyone you want right on the bill," Mr. Greene explained.

Sure enough, as the kids examined the bill they recognized the face in the center. It was Mr. Letterman, the printer.

"He's one of our first customers," said Mrs. Greene. "If he likes them, he's going to use Mug Money to help advertise his store."

"It seems," Phil Klink said calmly, "you've uncovered some *funny money* all right. *Play* money."

The Chief and Mrs. Klink apologized to the Greenes and led the children home.

The next day, as Wednesdays go, was the pits. In all of their combined years, the kids couldn't remember when they'd been more embarrassed.

It started right after lunch when Amy Farber came back to school. Amy always went home for lunch because her mother was a health nut and didn't like the school meals.

Amy was in Jimmy and Jay's homeroom class. When she came back from lunch, she was smiling. In ten minutes she'd told the whole class about the kids' mistake at the Greenes'.

It seemed her mother had talked to a neighbor, who had talked to another neighbor, who had talked to Mrs. Klink. Anyway, the story got around school, and by dismissal time the kids were famous . . . as clowns.

But by four o'clock things were looking a little better. Though Cosmic Cop hadn't saved the universe—in fact, he was trapped again—the trap sparked an idea in Jay's head.

"Can Cosmic Cop prove he isn't a cosmic counterfeiter?" boomed the voice of the TV announcer. "Or has Bad Penny Slade really framed our hero? Be with us tomorrow and see."

Jay leaped from the couch and turned off the set. "That's it!" he shouted. "That's what happened to us last night!"

"What are you talking about?" asked Jimmy.

"Just now Bad Penny Slade made Cosmic Cop look bad, right?" Jay asked enthusiastically.

"Sure," said Lee. "But—"

"I get it," said Dottie. "Because Cosmic *looks* like a crook, the galactic police won't believe anything he says about the *real* crooks."

"Right," Jay cheered. "And the Greenes did the same thing to us. They made *us* look bad."

"So now no one will believe us about the Greenes. No matter what we say." Jimmy smacked his fist into the palm of his hand.

"Are you sure the Greenes are really crooks?" asked Lee. "I mean, what if it *was* only play money T.J. and I saw?"

"Don't forget the first time we saw their money," said Jay, waving his finger in Lee's face. "It looked like real money to me. Besides, who hides play money in a duck?"

"He's right," said T.J., jumping up from his pillows. "And I just remembered. After Mr. Greene caught us last night, he took us into the house."

"So?" said Jimmy.

"Only *Mr.* Greene took us inside. Mrs. Greene didn't come inside until five minutes later!"

"Then she could have hidden the real phony money," said Lee. "I mean the phony real money. I mean the fake—oh, skip it!"

"So what do we do next?" T.J. asked.

"We get serious." There was a bright light in Jay's eyes.

"We start acting like real detectives," he continued. "We make a plan, we look for clues, we get evidence, we—"

"We give ourselves flashy code names!" T.J. interrupted.

"What for?" asked Jimmy. He was busily taking notes.

"Every good spy has a bunch of different disguises and tricks. You know, in case he gets in trouble, or has to hide, or the bad guys overhear his secret messages."

"We don't have any secret messages," Dottie sighed.

"Not *yet*," said T.J.

"I think it's a good idea," said Lee.

Jay shrugged his shoulders. "Okay. Code names it is."

A half hour later everyone had a code name. They were less than fear-inspiring.

"All right," Jay announced. "Here are the code names. Dottie is Short Stuff, Lee is Smudge—"

"Gee, thanks," Lee mumbled.

Jay grinned. "T.J. is Smoke Screen." T.J. gave a thumbs-up sign. "I'm Clicker and Jimmy is—"

"Jaws," Jimmy grumbled. "I can't believe you guys named me Jaws."

"Believe it," Dottie said with a smile. She turned to face the rest of the group. "Now, are we ready to take on the Greenes?"

Jay stood up from the couch. "Now we're ready. And tomorrow we start at the top."

"We split up and start grilling everybody involved, right?" asked Jimmy, rubbing his hands together.

"That's right," said Jay. "And you and Lee start with the big fish first. Mr. DeVidus Cashton, at the Dozerville First National Bank."

Being in the Dozerville bank at lunchtime was like trying to buy tickets for the World Series. There were tons of people on line, and all of them were in a hurry.

Jimmy and Lee watched as they stood by Mr. Cashton's desk. The boys had made it this far because his secretary knew Mrs. Klink. But once inside, they found out Mr. Cashton was out to lunch.

Jimmy had told the secretary that they wanted to leave him a note. So while she answered a phone call, Lee stood at the vice president's desk. But he wasn't writing a note. He was dusting one for fingerprints.

"Are you sure you know what you're doing?" Jimmy asked. He was standing lookout by the office door.

"Sure I do," Lee snapped. "All I have to do is put the fingerprint powder on an object the suspect has touched." He pulled a small jar of black powder from his jacket pocket. "Then I'll blow away the extra powder and use the special tape to pick up the print. Simple."

"Well, hurry up, then," said Jimmy.

"Hold your horses," said Lee. "All I have to do is pull this cap off, and—oops!"

As Jimmy turned around he had an idea of

what he would see. He wasn't disappointed. Mr. Cashton's desk was covered in black powder.

Lee gave Jimmy a weak grin. "Guess I used a little too much."

"Hurry and clean it off," Jimmy whispered through his teeth. "Before his secretary gets off the phone."

Lee began gently blowing the powder off the desk and onto the dark brown carpet.

As he watched his foster brother, Jimmy leaned closer to the office door. Luck was with them. The secretary was still on the phone.

Within a few seconds Lee was standing next to Jimmy. "I got some prints," he said, brushing dust off his jacket.

"Good." Jimmy looked at the dark spots on Lee's clothing and shook his head. "And you wondered why we called you Smudge."

Just as Lee was about to reply, a part of the secretary's conversation caught their attention.

"That's right, sweetheart," she said into the receiver. "I have to work late tomorrow—it's Friday, dear." There was another pause. "You know the armored truck always comes on Fridays. They're delivering a large shipment of money. Mr. Cashton and I have to handle all the paperwork by tomorrow at closing." Another pause. "Because after tomorrow Mr. Cashton is going on a long vacation."

Jimmy and Lee smiled. Now they were sure

they knew the link between the Greenes and Mr. Cashton.

"Thousands of dollars delivered to the bank, tomorrow—" Jimmy said softly.

"Thousands of phony dollars printed in a garage—" Lee added.

"They switch the money around—"

"And nobody will even know that the bank's been robbed!"

C·H·A·P·T·E·R
7

*J*immy and Lee could hardly wait to get back to school and tell the others what they'd uncovered.

Waving good-bye to the secretary, the boys hurried past guards, tellers, and customers, and rushed out of the bank.

"We've got to get back to school before the lunch period ends," said Jimmy. "Or we're in big trouble."

"So, let's move it!" Lee exclaimed.

Sneaker-clad feet pounded the streets that led back to the Wrighter Elementary School. Jimmy and Lee cut through the Oswald Knockworlder Memorial Park, and raced past J. J. Johnson's lumberyard.

They bounded up the school steps and through the doors just as the school bell rang.

As they headed for class, some of the other children snickered and whispered. Their schoolmates were still teasing them about the Greenes. But this time the boys didn't mind. They were on a case, and the pieces were beginning to fit.

At three-fifteen Jay and Dottie approached Mr. Letterman's printing store. Almost immediately Jay pulled out his flash camera and began shooting away.

He photographed the sidewalk, the alley that ran alongside the shop, and even the trash cans. *Click, click,* and *click.*

"You missed the doorknob," Dottie teased. *Click.*

Inside the shop Mr. Letterman was busy studying a poster design. He looked up and squinted as the kids approached the counter.

"What can I do for you youngsters?" he asked.

Dottie was ready. She pulled a sheet of paper from her notebook. "How much would a hundred copies of this cost?"

Mr. Letterman took the sheet of paper. "An advertisement, heh?" The printer smiled. "Would you like to see our selection of colored paper?"

"Just the price, sir," Dottie said.

The elderly printer adjusted his gold-rimmed glasses and read out loud. "Lost something valuable? Are crooks on your tail? Then call on us, we never fail. We're the Clues Kids, detectives for hire. Just give us a clue, and we'll never tire."

The sales pitch was followed by the Klinks' phone number and a crude drawing of a magnifying glass.

"What do you think, Mr. Letterman?" Jay quickly took a picture of the printer's reaction. The flash was blinding.

"I think it's amusing," Mr. Letterman said, blinking his eyes. "Do you expect a lot of business in our sleepy little town?"

"We already have a case," said Dottie.

"Yeah," said Jay. "We're checking the activities of a suspicious person, or persons—"

"Suspicious?" asked Mr. Letterman.

"Yes. Suspicious," Jay replied. *Click, flash* went his camera. "A suspicious person or persons seen in the vicinity of your shop."

"My shop?" Mr. Letterman raised an eyebrow.

Click, flash. Mr. Letterman looked annoyed.

"Yes," said Dottie. "Your store. This person or persons was wearing a trench coat and carrying"—Dottie paused for effect— "a manila envelope."

Jay leaned in close to the printer. "Yeah. A manila envelope. What do you think of that?"

Click, flash—right in Mr. Letterman's face.

A moment later Jay and Dottie were standing in front of the shop. Mr. Letterman, rubbing his eyes, had escorted them to the door. He'd suggested that they come back another day—without the camera.

"Do you think we learned anything in there, Short Stuff?" asked Jay.

"Yeah, Clicker." Dottie replied.

"What?"

"That Mr. Letterman doesn't like to have his picture taken."

Jay nodded in agreement. "Right. Let's go home."

Meanwhile, outside Forrest and Olive Greene's garage, a large cardboard box mumbled.

The box was standing next to a number of other boxes that had been emptied and discarded by the Greenes. The mumbling box contained T.J. Booker and a small tape recorder.

"Time, three twenty-six and seven seconds," T.J. whispered into the microphone. "Agent Smoke Screen in position outside the suspects' base of operation. I'm about to move in for a closer look."

T.J. took a peek through a small hole in the box. The garage door was wide open, and he could see Mr. Greene moving around inside. The coast looked clear.

But just as T.J. was about to move, Mrs. Greene leaned out the kitchen window.

"Forrest," she called out.

Mr. Greene came out of the garage, sipping a can of soda. "What is it, dear?" He took a few steps forward and stopped right next to T.J.'s hiding place.

"Marty in Tylerville said he'd be sending the rest of our things in a few days," said Mrs. Greene.

"Good," said her husband. "I'll need some of that stuff real soon."

"Also," Mrs. Greene continued, "Mr. Cashton called. He'll be here tomorrow to pick up his package."

Forrest Greene nodded to his wife as she closed the window. He took the last sip of his soda and dropped the can into T.J.'s box.

"I've got to work on this disguise," T.J. mumbled as the can fell beside him.

As T.J. sat there, something began to bother him.

It was something the Greenes had just said. But no matter how hard he tried, T.J. just couldn't put his finger on it.

Suddenly the sound of a heavy-duty truck pulling into the driveway reached T.J.'s ears.

"Afternoon, Mr. Greene," said a gruff voice. "We're here to pick up your trash."

"That's great," said Mr. Greene. "But we've got a lot of junk to get rid of. Are you sure your truck can handle all this?"

"Oh, sure," said the trash man. "We'll just throw these in the back and the truck will squash them like bugs."

T.J. felt a hand smack the side of his box. He swallowed hard. He could jump out and be caught by Mr. Greene, or he could be thrown into a trash compactor.

Either way, he was trapped.

C·H·A·P·T·E·R
8

*F*righteningvisionsflashed
through T.J.'s mind. Pancakes, mashed potatoes. He had to get out of the box. But how?

When it seemed as if he had no choice
other than to reveal himself, Mr. Greene spoke
again.

"If you'll wait just a minute," he said, "I'll
go get your money."

"Don't worry about it," the trash man of-
fered. "You can pay by check."

"No, thank you," came Mr. Greene's re-
sponse. "My wife and I prefer to pay in cash,
at least until we've settled in."

The trash man smacked the top of the box.
"Suit yourself," he said. "My partner and I
will start with these boxes."

T.J. peeked through the hole. Mr. Greene was walking into the garage, and the trash man was standing with his back to the box. It was now or never.

T.J. tiptoed away from the garage and hurried along the hedges. He popped his head out of the box only long enough to see if any cars were coming, then bolted across the street.

As T.J. crossed his front lawn, he could hear the trash man shouting to his partner. "Come on, Marty. Where is it? Boxes just don't walk away."

"They do if they're a top disguise artist named Smoke Screen," T.J. said softly. He let out a long, low chuckle as he disappeared into the clubhouse.

When the other kids came home they found a note on the television set. It reminded them that they were being punished. Aside from increased chores and early curfew, no *Cosmic Cop*. They groaned, then shuffled out to the clubhouse.

They found T.J., still in his cardboard disguise, waiting for them. He gave his report as quickly as he could. And he made sure to mention escaping from the diabolical compactor of doom.

"I was smooth," said T.J., stepping out of the box. He put on a pair of dark glasses and pretended to brush lint from his clothes. "I was cool. I was fast. I was—"

"You were lucky," said Dottie angrily.

"Hey," T.J. countered. "I got away."

"But you could have been hurt!" Dottie shouted.

"Well, what do you care?" asked T.J.

"I do! Okay?" said Dottie.

"Okay," T.J. said softly. He tossed his glasses on the desk.

"So," said Jimmy, checking his notes, "some guy from Tylerville is going to send the rest of the Greenes' furniture. Right?"

"Yup," said T.J.

"And Mr. Cashton is coming over tomorrow to pick something up?"

"Double yup." T.J. scratched his head. "You know—something's been bothering me, something I've been trying to remember. It's about the Greenes."

"Keep trying," said Jay, patting T.J. on the shoulder. "Meanwhile, we need a few things."

"Like what?" asked Jimmy, his pencil poised over his notepad.

"We need the Greenes' fingerprints," said Jay. "And we've got to find out all we can about counterfeiting."

Lee snapped his fingers. "How about asking the Dozerville police? They'd know if there were counterfeiters in the area."

"The *Dozerville Herald* had a big story on counterfeiting," Dottie said eagerly. "I remember the Chief reading about it last week."

"He's probably thrown it away by now," said Lee.

"But we could get a copy at the newspaper office." Jimmy jumped up. "I could even talk to their ace reporter, Tabby Lloyd."

"That's great," said Jay. "Then here's the plan. Jimmy and T.J.—"

"Use our code names," T.J. insisted.

Jay sighed. "All right. Jaws and Smoke Screen will go to the newspaper office. I'll go to the police station. Some of the chief's friends might know something. And Short Stuff and Smudge will try to get the Greenes' fingerprints."

Jimmy looked up from his notepad. "Got it," he said. "Only problem is, we have to do all this before we come home tomorrow. We're kind of grounded, remember?"

"We'll do it!" Lee said with determination.

The kids cheered and gave a thumbs-up. All five of them were ready to fight crime in the streets.

"Kids," Phil Klink called from the kitchen. "Get in here. It's KP time!"

Crime in the streets would have to wait.

Friday afternoon from three to three-thirty Dozerville seemed under attack by a small tornado. The kids were everywhere—like mosquitoes.

Lee and Dottie went over to the Greenes' home carrying a plate of cookies and a pitcher of milk. They claimed they'd come to apologize for everything. The Greenes were tickled pink.

For fifteen minutes the kids talked about

everything they could think of. Dottie pretended to be interested in everyplace the Greenes had ever been and in everything they had ever done. While Dottie smiled and chattered, Lee kept trying to pull out his kit and get a print. But somehow the Greenes were always there—always watching. Mrs. Greene even washed the dishes they brought. "Can't have you taking dirty dishes home," she said.

The kids were friendly, funny, and polite. And when that failed, they broke something.

"I'll get a wastebasket," said Mr. Greene, shaking his head. He went out to the kitchen.

"I'm sorry," said Lee as he stood over the broken flowerpot. "It was—an accident."

Mrs. Greene tried to smile. "Don't worry about it. After what the movers broke, this is nothing." She bent down and started picking up some of the clay pieces.

When Mr. Greene returned, Lee and Dottie knelt down to help. And as soon as the Greenes weren't looking, Lee slipped a couple of the broken pieces into his pocket—pieces the Greenes had touched.

"Well," said Mrs. Greene when she stood up, "that should do it."

"Yes," said Dottie, smiling at Lee. "That should *really* do it."

Jay's trip to the police station was short and sweet. He didn't have to ask a single question.

As he walked into the station he spotted an

angry man yelling at the desk sergeant. Jay recognized the man as a store owner from the downtown area.

He was waving a twenty-dollar bill and yelling.

"The people at my bank tell me it's phony, a fake!" he shouted. "I've got six more of these bills! Now, what are you going to do about it?"

Jay raised his camera and smiled. *Click, flash.* "Mr. and Mrs. Greene, I gotcha."

The score was Clues Kids two, Greenes nothing as Jimmy and T.J. walked into the offices of the *Dozerville Herald.*

They spotted Tabby Lloyd sitting at the far side of the pressroom. She was bent over her computer, typing like crazy.

At twenty-two years old, Tabby Lloyd was the youngest reporter on the paper. She planned to become the best. The Clues Kids hadn't exactly been a help to her career. Although Jimmy had called in a number of—well—*tips*, they'd turned out to be less than accurate.

So when Tabby saw Jimmy and T.J. walking toward her, she wasn't jumping for joy. But at least she didn't try to hide.

"Hello, T.J.," said the reporter, running her fingers through her long, frizzy hair. T.J. nodded.

"And if it isn't my favorite roving reporter, Jimmy Locke," Tabby chuckled.

"Hi, Miss Lloyd," Jimmy said cheerfully.

"What are you reporting today? Spies operating out of the local ice cream parlor? Or another escaped convict hiding in the town zoo?"

Jimmy lowered his head. "I'm sorry about that zoo story tip. I really thought I saw the convict go into the elephant house."

"The reporter who covered that story still isn't talking to me," said Tabby. "Anyway, what can I do for you today?"

Jimmy cleared his throat. "We need to see an article that your paper ran a week ago."

"It was all about counterfeiters," T.J. added. "Do you know anything about it?"

"I should," said the reporter. "I wrote it. What do you need to know?"

"Everything." T.J. flashed a big smile.

"Especially how they operate," said Jimmy. He pulled out his pen and notepad. "You know, how they make the money. Where they spend it. Stuff like that."

"Why?" Tabby asked.

"Nothing much," Jimmy mumbled. "We're just curious."

"Uh-huh." Tabby Lloyd leaned back in her chair and began nibbling on a pencil. "I'll tell you a few things," she said finally. "Then I'll give you a copy of the article."

"Great," the boys said eagerly.

Tabby smiled. "Okay, a counterfeiter uses plates to make phony money. A plate is like a negative, except it's made of metal. It has the image of the dollar bill they're faking carved right into it."

Jimmy was writing feverishly. "How do they spread the bills around?" he asked, never looking up from his notes.

"Most counterfeiters simply spend it around town," Tabby replied. "They just—buy things."

"Do they disguise themselves?" T.J. asked.

A slight smile appeared on the reporter's face. "T.J., they usually look like plain, ordinary people."

"This is great stuff," said Jimmy, tapping his notes. "We just have one more question." He and T.J. leaned toward Tabby. "Have there been any counterfeiters in this area recently?"

"As a matter of fact," Tabby replied, "there was a rash of counterfeit money appearing not far from here. But that stopped about a month ago."

"Did the police catch the counterfeiters?" asked T.J.

"No," Tabby said sadly. "They just disappeared."

"Do you remember where they struck last?" asked Jimmy.

The young reporter closed her eyes for a second. Then she said, "Yes, I do. It was a nice little town a few miles away. I think it was called Tylerville."

Jimmy and T.J.'s eyes widened. Suddenly this one piece of news made everything seem real.

The counterfeiters had struck in Tylerville,

then disappeared. Maybe the police didn't know where they were, but the Clues Kids did. Now all they had to do was prove it.

C·H·A·P·T·E·R
9

"*T*hank you, Miss Lloyd," said Jimmy, shaking Tabby's hand wildly. "That's the best news we've ever heard."

The reporter looked confused. "You're welcome. But what did I— "

"We've got to go now," said T.J. as he raced across the room. "Thanks again!"

"Don't you want a copy of the article?" Tabby called out.

"No, thank you," said Jimmy. He stopped as he reached the door. "We've got everything we need. Bye!"

In a flash the boys were gone. Tabby Lloyd sat wondering what they were up to. The young reporter wasn't sure why, but she had the feeling something big was about to happen.

She was right.

By five-thirty the clubhouse was a beehive of activity.

Jay stood in front of a large drawing pad. The pad was attached to the wall with four long pushpins. On one sheet of paper Jay and Jimmy had written down everything they knew about the case. In the past hour that had turned into a lot.

"Okay," said Jay. "Let's look at what we have. There were counterfeiters in a town called Tylerville."

"And the Greenes come from Tylerville," said T.J. "Not Walkerton, like the Chief thought. That's what I was trying to remember before."

"Good," Jay continued. "Next—"

"I know I saw real money in their duck," Dottie declared.

"We all saw it," Jay said. "And on the day we followed Mrs. Greene, she spent money all over the downtown area."

"And that's where the store owner came from," said Jimmy, checking his notes. "The one Jay saw at the police station, waving the funny money."

Lee jumped up from the floor. "And Tabby Lloyd said that's how counterfeiters spread their funny money! They spend it around town!"

"Right." Jay checked that on their list. "Now, Dottie and Lee got the Greenes' fingerprints. We could give them to the Chief and he could see if they have a record."

Jimmy noticed Dottie was frowning. "What's wrong?" he asked.

"We don't have any real evidence," she said quietly. "We don't have the pans."

"You mean the plates," T.J. said with a smile.

"Right," said Dottie. "And without proof, we can't stop them."

"That's true," said Jay. "But we have enough to show the Chief."

"And maybe he can get a search warrant," Lee added.

Jimmy stood up and raised his pencil over his head. "With the information we've gathered, the Chief can't possibly ignore us now. He'll see we were right!" He puffed out his chest. "I'm serious, the Chief won't turn us down this time."

"No," Phil Klink said calmly. The whole family was gathered in the living room. "I won't take this to the police."

"But, Chief," Lee pleaded. "We know we're right . . . this time."

Patty Klink sat forward in her recliner. She placed her hands on Jimmy's and Lee's shoulders. "Do you remember when you all first came here? Do you remember how you mistrusted everyone?"

Lee lowered his head. "That was different. We didn't know anyone."

"We didn't even know you." Jimmy looked into Mrs. Klink's eyes. "We were scared."

"That's true," said Phil Klink. "Just like you are now."

"Honest, Chief," Jay pleaded. "This is different. You and Mrs. Klink taught us to trust people, and to trust you."

Dottie put her arms around Phil Klink and hugged him as hard as she could. "Please believe us, Chief. The Greenes are bad—and you've got to stop them."

Phil and Patty exchanged long glances, then Phil let out a big sigh. "All right," he said, rising from his chair. "I guess it can't hurt to check around."

"Hooray!" the kids cheered.

"But," Phil said, raising his hand for silence, "I promise nothing. Without evidence there's no case. And right now there isn't even a speck."

When the kids heard Phil's car pull out of the driveway, they didn't feel like cheering.

"He's right," Jay said, disgusted. "We don't have any hard evidence."

There was a feeling of sadness in Jay's room. He and the other kids sat in the dark, staring at the Greenes' house.

"It's almost seven o'clock," said Lee. "That's when Mr. Cashton said he was going to show up at the house."

"We don't even know if he's part of the gang or not." Jimmy sighed.

"I don't think he is," said Dottie. She was sitting on Jay's bed, hugging one of her stuffed animals. "I've always trusted Mr. Cashton."

"Well, the Greenes might be planning to do something to him," Lee suggested.

Jay suddenly went to the closet and grabbed his jacket. "We're not going to find out sitting here."

"Have you got a plan?" asked T.J.

"I sure do," Jay replied. "Are you with me?"

Lee smiled. "Will this keep us from doing our homework?"

"For a little while," Jay replied.

"Then we're with you!" The kids cheered, but softly. They didn't want Mrs. Klink to hear them.

"Okay," Jay said, gathering them into a huddle. "Here's what we do."

Seven o'clock on a Friday night is usually a pretty quiet time in Dozerville. The Clues Kids were about to change that.

By the light of the moon three figures crawled along the hedges near the Greenes' garage. First Jay, loaded with cameras, then Lee, carrying his super deluxe fingerprinting kit, and T.J., dressed like a pony express rider. It was the only disguise that was clean.

The boys had just made it to the dark side of the garage when Mr. Cashton's car pulled up. In a few minutes the banker had disappeared into the house.

"Now's our chance," Jay whispered. "We've got to sneak into the garage and find those plates."

"What makes you think they're in there?" T.J. asked.

"Because I read a detective story once," Jay replied. "And it said, 'The best place to hide something is in plain sight.' "

"So let's get inside that garage," said Lee.

Suddenly T.J. grabbed Jay's jacket. "What if we get caught?"

"Don't worry," Jay said calmly. "Dottie and Jimmy are watching. If anything happens, they'll call for backup."

"That didn't work the last time," T.J. commented.

"I wasn't with you," Jay growled. "Now, come on."

Quickly and quietly this time, the boys made their way into the garage.

Once inside, they each pulled out a flashlight and began searching. For the first five minutes all they found were tools, old clothing, and stacks of books. It wasn't until they reached the printing press that things got interesting.

"What's this?" asked Jay. He was holding up a rubber rectangle about the size of a small book.

"It looks like the stamper they use to make the Mug Money," said Lee. He shone his light across the table, then stopped when he saw something behind the copier.

"Look," he said. "Here are a few more."

"In plain sight," Jay mumbled.

"What?" T.J. asked.

Jay grabbed all the stampers and began examining them. At first he found nothing unusual. Then, on the very last one, he hit pay dirt.

"This one's heavier than the others," Jay whispered excitedly. "Look, guys—it comes apart."

Sure enough, the thick rubber stamper broke in half. Hidden inside were two thin metal shapes, about six inches long. And etched into the metal was the image of a twenty-dollar bill.

"The plates," Lee whispered, jumping up and down. "We found the plates! I bet the Greenes' prints are all over them!"

"Take it easy," Jay warned. "Now all we have to do is get one of these to the Chief."

"Why only one?" Lee asked.

"Because the police have to find some evidence at the scene of the crime," Jay explained.

"Otherwise the Greenes could get away again," T.J. added.

"Now let's get out of here," said Jay as he carefully slipped one of the plates into his pocket. "We've got one more thing to do."

C·H·A·P·T·E·R
10

*F*rom Jay's bedroom window Jimmy and Dottie watched as their teammates came out of the garage. Jay aimed his flashlight at the window and blinked it three times.

"They found the plates," Jimmy and Dottie cheered.

"Now," said Jimmy, checking his list, "all they have to do is take a picture of the Greenes with Mr. Cashton."

"But what if he *isn't* a crook?" asked Dottie.

"Then, um, uh, we'll give him a copy for his office wall," Jimmy stuttered.

"Very funny," said Dottie. "What are they doing now?"

Jimmy raised the binoculars to his eyes. "As far as I can tell . . . they're creeping past the garage. Now they're sneaking up to the house. Good. Now they're peeking into the window. Fantastic! Jay's pulled out his camera . . . he's taking a picture . . . they're backing away from the window, and—oops."

"What do you mean, 'oops'?" asked Dottie.

"I mean Mr. Greene just grabbed them," Jimmy replied, throwing down the binoculars. "Come on! We've got to get over there!"

"Look what I found," Mr. Greene announced as he walked through the front door of his house. He had a firm grip on Lee and was pushing Jay and T.J. ahead of him. "I *thought* I saw lights in the garage."

Mr. Cashton looked very confused. "Aren't those three of the Klinks' kids?"

"It seems," said Mrs. Greene, "these children just love to visit us—in the dark."

"You'd better let us go," said Jay. "We've got friends hidden outside."

"Yeah. If anything happens to us," said T.J., "they'll call the cops."

"They're probably calling them right now," Lee said smugly. "So you might as well give up."

Just then Dottie and Jimmy came running through the front door and into the middle of the room.

"Okay, freeze!" Jimmy yelled.

Mr. Greene smiled as he closed the door. "Are these your *hidden* friends?"

"Tell me you called the police," Jay pleaded to his brother.

"Well, I—"

"Tell me you told Mrs. Klink where you were going."

"Well, we—uh, we—uh—"

"What is the meaning of this?" asked Mr. Cashton.

Dottie ran to the banker's side. "These people are counterfeiters, and we thought you were, too, but I don't think so anymore, because I trust you and your bank. I know you're not a crook—are you?"

Mr. Greene smiled. "These children mistook our Mug Money for the real thing," he explained.

Mr. Cashton started laughing. "Is that it? Well, Dottie, I just bought some Mug Money as a gift for my wife. See?" he said, holding up one of the packets. "That's her picture in the center."

"Is that what you gave Mrs. Greene the other day?" asked Dottie. "A picture of your wife?"

"That's correct," the banker replied.

Mrs. Greene sighed heavily. "We've had a talk with their parents already. But it looks like we'll have to do it again."

"You sure will," Jay exclaimed. "Especially when they see this!" Jay pulled the plate from his pocket and showed it to Mr. Cashton.

The banker was shocked. "This looks like the real thing." He examined the plate closely. "It *is* the real thing! Where did you get this?"

T.J. pointed at the Greenes. "From a secret place in their garage!"

Before anyone could move, Mr. Greene grabbed the plate and pushed Mr. Cashton away. The friendly expression had left his face. Now he and his wife looked really angry—and very dangerous.

"You had to keep snooping, didn't you?" Mrs. Greene snarled. "Well, since you've found out our little secret, we'll have to do something unpleasant."

"Take away our TV privileges?" Jimmy asked with a nervous chuckle.

"I'm afraid it'll be much more unpleasant than that," Mr. Greene replied. "Get some rope, Olive. And we'll—"

Suddenly the roar of a police bullhorn ripped through the quiet. "This is the police!" came a familiar voice. "You are ordered to surrender at once!"

"It's the Chief!" Jimmy shouted.

"Mr. and Mrs. Greene," Dottie shouted. "You're hash!"

Panic washed across the Greenes' faces. They looked like cornered rats.

"I don't believe this!" Mr. Greene shouted.

"What do we do?" asked Mrs. Greene. She stood near Dottie, biting her nails.

Just then, Jay and Jimmy noticed Mr. Greene was standing on a small rug. Jay shouted, "Flying carpet!"

Moving together, the twins dropped to the floor, grabbed one end of the rug, and yanked as hard as they could. Forrest Greene went flying, feet over head. He landed, very hard, on the wooden coffee table, right in the middle of a plate of cheese dip.

Dottie ran across the room and whipped open the front door. "Come and get them!"

The Chief, Mrs. Klink, and two police officers came running into the house—followed by Tabby Lloyd. Mrs. Greene looked from her husband to the two police officers—and fainted.

Lee looked up at Phil Klink and smiled. "Book 'em, Chief. Book 'em."

There were hugs all around.

Twenty minutes later the kids had told their story to Tabby Lloyd and the chief. Then it was Phil Klink's turn to explain.

"You should thank Miss Lloyd too, kids," he said. "She was down at the station asking the same questions I was."

"Really?" said Jimmy.

The reporter smiled. "That's right. Your visit got me thinking, so I started asking around."

"We found out pretty much the same things you did," Phil continued. "So I got the police to come over to talk to the Greenes."

"And I decided to tag along," said Tabby. "When we arrived, your mother flagged us down, and told us what was going on."

The kids looked stunned. "How did you know?" Jay asked.

Mrs. Klink smiled. "You don't think you're the only kids to sneak out of a house, do you? I saw Jimmy and Dottie run over here. I fol-

lowed them, and arrived in time to hear Mr. Greene's little confession."

"Well, that about rounds it up," said Tabby Lloyd. "I've got a story to write."

"Will we be in it?" Jimmy asked.

Tabby laughed as she turned off her tape recorder. "Kids, you *are* the story."

"We're going to be in the papers," Lee cheered.

"We're going to be heroes," Jay added.

"We're going to be detectives," shouted T.J.

"We're going to be grounded again." Dottie sighed. She was looking at the Klinks' faces.

"That's right," Mrs. Klink said with a smile. "You did a wonderful job catching these crooks, but you took some very dangerous chances. I'm afraid you'll have to spend some time in our version of *the clink*."

Despite what their foster parents had said, the kids walked home with their heads held high. Jimmy, Jay, Lee, T.J., and Dottie were proud of themselves. With skill and a great deal of dumb luck they had solved their first case. For now, thanks to them, the world— well, at least their town—was safe.

This is Dozerville, population 12,533 and a half. For a few days it was 12,535 and a half, but two people are about to get room and board elsewhere.

And in some darkened hideout, a new villain is about to embark on a plan to bring fear to the hearts of these citizens.

But that's another story, in the next adventure of . . . The Clues Kids.